D1543325

The Adventures of Franklin and Friends

A Collection of 8 Stories

Kids Can Press

From eight episodes of the animated TV series *Franklin and Friends*, produced by Nelvana Limited/Infinite Frameworks Pte. Ltd.
Based on the Franklin books by Paulette Bourgeois and Brenda Clark.

Franklin is a trademark of Kids Can Press Ltd.

The character Franklin was created by Paulette Bourgeois and Brenda Clark.

The Adventures of Franklin and Friends: A Collection of 8 Stories © 2013 Contextx Inc. and Brenda Clark Illustrator Inc.

This book includes the following stories first published in 2012:

Franklin and the Big Small Case, based on the TV episode *The Super Clupers' Big Small Case*, written by Lienne Sawatsky and Dan Williams

Franklin and the Gecko Games, based on the TV episode *Franklin and the Gecko Games*, written by Karen Moonah

Franklin and the Wonder, based on the TV episode *Franklin and the Wonder*, written by Cathy Moss

Franklin in the Stars, based on the TV episode *Franklin in the Stars*, written by James R. Backshall

Franklin, the Little Bubble, based on the TV episode *Franklin, the Little Bubble*, written by Jeff Sweeny

Franklin's Partner, based on the TV episode *Franklin's Partner*, written by Jeff Sweeny

Franklin's Spaceship, based on the TV episode *Franklin's Spaceship*, written by James R. Backshall

Franklin's Ups and Downs, based on the TV episode *Franklin's Ups and Downs*, written by Ursula Ziegler-Sullivan

All TV tie-in adaptations written by Harry Endrulat.
All text © 2012 Contextx Inc.
All illustrations © 2012 Brenda Clark Illustrator Inc.

All rights reserved. No part of this publication may be reproduced, stored in a retrieval system or transmitted, in any form or by any means, without the prior written permission of Kids Can Press Ltd. or, in case of photocopying or other reprographic copying, a license from The Canadian Copyright Licensing Agency (Access Copyright). For an Access Copyright license, visit www.accesscopyright.ca or call toll free to 1-800-893-5777.

App Store is a service mark of Apple Inc.

Treehouse logo is a trademark™ of Corus™ Entertainment group of companies. All rights reserved.

Nick Jr. and all related titles, logos and characters are trademarks of Viacom International Inc.

Kids Can Press acknowledges the financial support of the Ontario Arts Council, the Canada Council for the Arts and the Government of Canada, through the CBF, for our publishing activity.

Published in Canada by
Kids Can Press Ltd.
25 Dockside Drive
Toronto, ON M5A 0B5
www.kidscanpress.com

Published in the U.S. by
Kids Can Press Ltd.
2250 Military Road
Tonawanda, NY 14150

This book is smyth sewn casebound.

Manufactured in Shenzhen, China, in 4/2013 by C&C Offset

CM 13 0 9 8 7 6 5 4 3 2 1

Library and Archives Canada Cataloguing in Publication

Endrulat, Harry
    The adventures of Franklin and friends :
a collection of 8 stories / written by Harry Endrulat.

(Franklin and friends)
Based on the character by Paulette Bourgeois and Brenda Clark.

Contents: Franklin and the wonder — Franklin, the little bubble — Franklin and the big small case — Franklin's partner — Franklin's spaceship — Franklin's ups and downs — Franklin in the stars — Franklin and the gecko games.

ISBN 978-1-77138-027-0

    1. Franklin (Fictitious character : Bourgeois) — Juvenile fiction. I. Bourgeois, Paulette II. Clark, Brenda III. Title. IV. Series: Franklin and friends

PS8609.N37A64 2013   jC813'.6   C2013-901897-2

Kids Can Press is a *corus*™ Entertainment company

Contents

Franklin
and the Wonder

6

FRANKLIN and his friends liked going to school. Their teacher, Mr. Owl, helped them learn to read and write. He taught them math and science and art.

One day, Mr. Owl took the class outside so they could learn about nature.

In the schoolyard, the students found a spiderweb.

"What are webs made of?" asked Franklin.

"Spiders spin their webs out of long strands of silk," said Mr. Owl. "This web is just one example of the wonders of nature all around us!"

"Cool-io!" said Franklin.

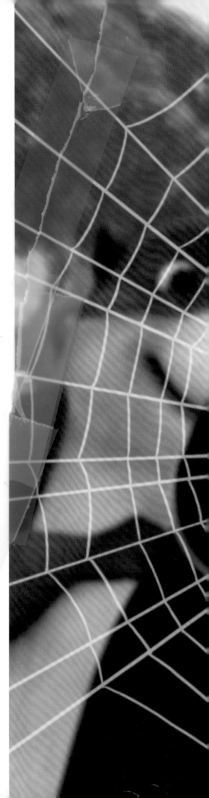

"For our next project, I'd like everyone to find a wonder of nature to show the class," said Mr. Owl.

"What's a wonder of nature?" asked Goose.

"It's anything wonderful, amazing or beautiful in nature," said Mr. Owl.

"Oh, like a rainbow," said Goose.

"Or a sunset," added Snail.

"Exactly!" said Mr. Owl.

Mr. Owl paired everyone up. Franklin was partnered with Rabbit.

"Remember," added Mr. Owl, "each partner will speak about the wonder and be ready to answer questions."

Rabbit gasped. "Speak in front of everybody?"

"Come on, Rabbit," said Franklin. He couldn't wait to get started. But Rabbit wasn't so eager.

Franklin and Rabbit walked into the woods. They found a bush with a strange green object hanging from a branch.

"Neat, neat, neat!" said Rabbit.

"What do you think it is?" asked Franklin.

"Something *you* can talk about in front of the class," said Rabbit nervously.

"I think we found our wonder of nature," said Franklin, carefully breaking off the branch. "Maybe Aunt T knows what it is."

Franklin and Rabbit ran to Aunt T's house. Inside, Mr. Mole was having his portrait painted.

"Hey, what do you have there?" asked Aunt T.

"We were looking for a wonder of nature to show the class and found this. Do you know what it is?" asked Franklin.

"I certainly do," said Mr. Mole. "It's a chrysalis."

"What's a chrysalis?" asked Franklin.

"Well, a chrysalis is a little bed that a caterpillar makes for himself," said Mr. Mole. "He goes inside for a time, and when he comes out again, he has turned into a butterfly."

"Just like those butterflies in the garden," said Aunt T, pointing to the ones outside the window.

"This is the best wonder of nature ever!" said Franklin. "Come on, Rabbit. Let's get to work on our show and tell."

On the day of the presentations, Franklin and Rabbit listened as the other students talked about their wonders.

But when it was finally their turn, Rabbit was nowhere to be found!

Franklin searched everywhere. At last, he found Rabbit on the swings.

"Why did you leave before our show and tell?" asked Franklin.

"Because I was afraid," said Rabbit.

"Afraid? Of what?" asked Franklin.

"Of talking in front of the class," said Rabbit. "I'm afraid everyone will laugh at me."

23

Franklin thought for a moment. "Sometimes when I'm scared, practicing what scares me helps."

But Rabbit was too scared to practice talking in front of anyone. That gave Franklin an idea.

Franklin took Rabbit to Aunt T's house. The three of them painted pictures of everyone in the class. Then Rabbit practiced speaking to the paintings.

Later that day, Franklin and Rabbit did their show and tell. Just as they were finishing, the chrysalis began to move. It began to shake.

Suddenly, a butterfly emerged and flew into the sky!
Everyone in the class clapped.
"Excellent!" said Mr. Owl.

Rabbit let out a big sigh of relief.

"You did great," Franklin told Rabbit.

"Thanks, Franklin," said Rabbit. "I think we *both* did great!"

Franklin, the Little Bubble

FRANKLIN and his friends loved to visit
Aunt T at her Messy Make-It Shop. She always
had fun and exciting things for them to do.
They might paint pictures, splash in water —
or even stomp in mud!

One day, Franklin and his friends were playing outside the shop when something strange happened.

Tiny bubbles started floating their way! A minute later, they heard a shout from inside.

"Oh, no!" Aunt T shouted.

"Aunt T is in trouble," said Franklin. "Come on!"

Inside the shop, a strange machine was blowing bubbles.
"What's going on?" asked Franklin.

"It's the bubble maker I bought for my party tomorrow,"
said Aunt T. "It's going too fast!"

Franklin took a close look at the machine. A bubble landed on his nose and popped! Franklin jumped and accidentally bumped the bubble maker. The machine chugged to a stop.

"Thanks, my Little Bubble," said Aunt T, giving Franklin a hug. "I had better go open some windows to let these bubbles out."

After Aunt T left, Fox and Rabbit made fun of Franklin's new name.

"Fox and I have to go home now," said Rabbit. "Bye, Little Bubble."

"Yeah, bye, Little Bubble," giggled Fox. Franklin frowned as they walked away.

"I don't think that's funny," Franklin said.

"Those guys are just kidding around," said Snail.

"It isn't just that," said Franklin. "It's Aunt T. She's always calling me strange names."

It wasn't long before Aunt T came back. She scooped up a poster she had made earlier.

"I have to go hang this up to let everyone know about the party," Aunt T said. "I'm having it here at the Messy Make-It Shop."

"Neat!" said Snail.

"See you both at the party tomorrow," said Aunt T, walking toward town.

"I can't wait!" said Snail. "Everybody will be there."

"Oh, no," said Franklin. "Aunt T is sure to call me her Little Bubble. Snail, you have to help me."

"Help you do what?" asked Snail.

"I have an idea, but we have to hurry," said Franklin.

Franklin and Snail followed Aunt T. They watched from the bushes as she hung up the poster.

"We can't take your aunt's poster, Franklin," whispered Snail. "That would be wrong."

"We're not going to. We'll just make sure no one reads it," replied Franklin.

After Aunt T left, Franklin and Snail got some balloons. They stood in front of the poster so no one could see it.

That night, Franklin felt relieved. No one knew about the party. And no one would know about his silly nickname.

The next day, Aunt T asked Franklin to bring over some paintbrushes. Bear and Snail went with him.

"Hey, my Little Bubble," said Aunt T. "Thanks for bringing the brushes."

Aunt T and Snail took the brushes over to the painting area.

"Did she just call you her Little Bubble?" asked Bear with a chuckle.

"What's so funny about that?" said Franklin, as they wandered over to join Snail.

"It just reminds me of my mom," said Bear. "She always calls me Honey Pot."

"Doesn't it bother you?" asked Franklin.

"No. It just means that Mom cares about me," said Bear.

"I never thought about it that way," said Franklin. That's when he realized that Aunt T's silly nickname wasn't silly at all. It meant that she loved him.

"Uh-oh," said Franklin. "Nobody knows about the party. I have to tell Aunt T."

Franklin found Aunt T inside and told her what he had done.

"Why?" she asked.

"I didn't want anyone to hear you call me Little Bubble. Fox and Rabbit laughed at me," said Franklin. "Are you mad?"

"Of course not," said Aunt T. "I can stop calling you Little Bubble if you want."

"That's okay," said Franklin. "I like being your Little Bubble now."

"Okay then," said Aunt T with a smile. "But how do we get people to come to my party?"

Franklin thought and thought. Then he had an idea.

Aunt T started her bubble machine. She sent bubbles floating into town.

Bear took Snail to see Mrs. Periwinkle, who flew Snail all over town in her little plane. Snail told everyone to follow the bubbles.

Soon the Messy Make-It Shop was full of people. Even Fox and Rabbit came and painted pictures.

"Look, Franklin," said Rabbit, pointing to the sky. "A little bubble, just like you."

Aunt T came by and gave Fox and Rabbit a hug.

"What brilliant pictures, my Little Bubbles," she said to them.

Fox and Rabbit were speechless.

"Don't worry, my Little Bubbles," said Franklin with a laugh.

"It just means that she really cares about you!"

Franklin
and the Big Small Case

FRANKLIN and his friends liked to play detectives. Together, they searched for clues to solve mysteries. They called themselves the Super Cluepers.

One day, when they were playing in the yard, they heard Harriet yelling, "Help! Help!"

"This sounds like a job for the Super Cluepers!" said Franklin. He and his friends immediately changed into their super detective selves.

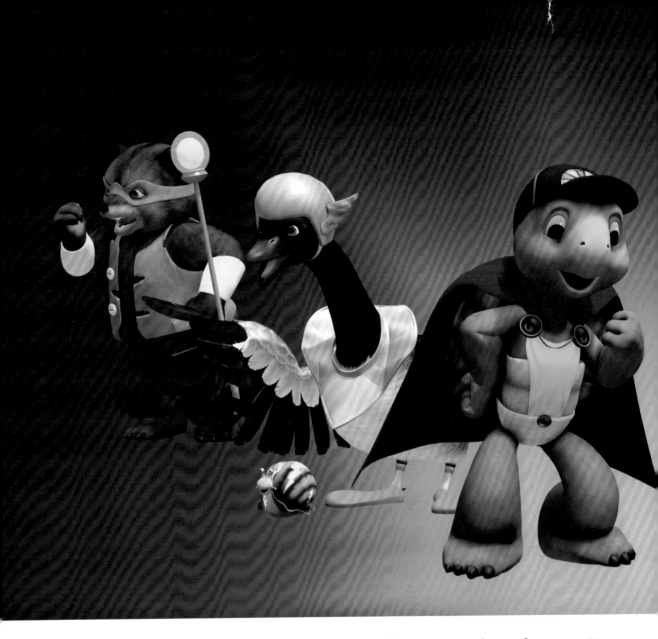

"Mega Bear is my name," said Bear. "With my cupcakes of power, I'm stronger than anybody!"

"With a voice like thunder, I'm no other than Thunder Boy!" said Snail.

"I'm Galaxy Gal, the magic girl with the magic wand!" said Goose.

"And I'm Green Wonder!" said Franklin.

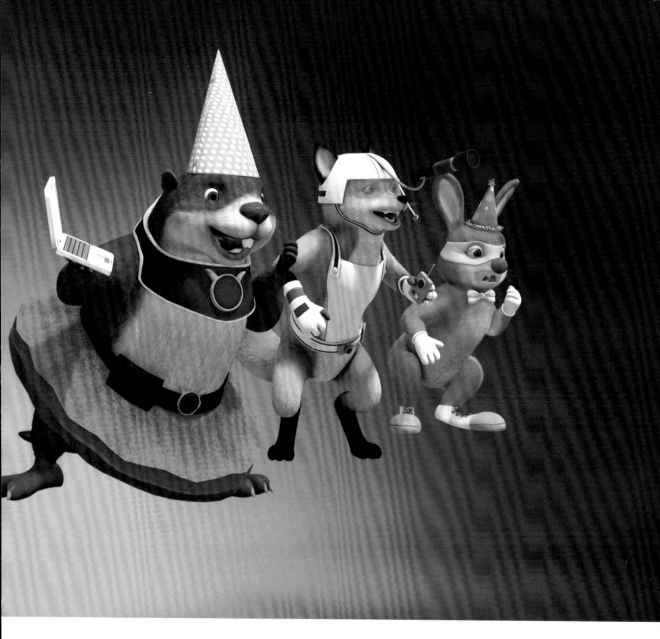

"I'm Book Whiz, the smartest of the smarts!" said Beaver.

"Everyone calls me Kid Gizmo," said Fox. "I'm the greatest gadget guy in the world!"

"I'm Giggler, the funniest kid ever!" said Rabbit.

The Super Cluepers found Harriet by the house.

"Super Cluepers," said Harriet, "I can't find Lilly Kitty anywhere. Will you help me?"

"Let's Super Clueper do it!" said Green Wonder.

The Super Cluepers decided to retrace Harriet's steps.

"Harriet, where were you right before we found you?" asked Galaxy Gal.

"At a tea party," said Harriet.

"Aha!" exclaimed Giggler. "Our first clue. Let's go!"

The Super Cluepers followed Harriet to the living room.

Kid Gizmo pulled out his special X-ray scope. He looked around the room.

"This is where Harriet's tea party was," said Kid Gizmo. "But I don't see Lilly Kitty anywhere."

Thunder Boy crawled out from under a tea towel. "I found another clue!" he said. "Look over here!"

The Super Cluepers gathered around. When Green Wonder pulled the tea towel away, he found muddy footprints.

Green Wonder bent down to get a closer look. "They're just like mine, but smaller," he observed.

"Are they Harriet's?" asked Giggler.

"They're Harriet's all right," said Green Wonder. "Good clue finding, Thunder Boy. Book Whiz, write this clue down!"

Book Whiz drew the footprint in her clue book. Then she noticed something else.

"Look! There's more!" Book Whiz said, pointing to a long trail of muddy footprints.

The Super Cluepers followed the footprints outside. They led to the vegetable garden and then suddenly stopped. A hose was on the ground, and there was mud all around.

"Now I remember!" said Green Wonder. "Harriet was helping my mom pick lettuce this morning."

"Harriet must have gotten her feet dirty here and walked inside for the tea party," said Book Whiz.

"It also means she could have left Lilly Kitty somewhere near the garden," added Green Wonder.

"Let's look around," said Galaxy Gal.

The Super Cluepers searched the garden. They didn't find Lilly Kitty. But they did find a piece of paper with a drawing on it.

"What is it?" asked Mega Bear.

Kid Gizmo zoomed in with his Super Eye. "It's a gumball machine," he declared.

"Where is there a gumball machine?" asked Thunder Boy.

"There's one in front of Mr. Mole's store," said Book Whiz. "Everybody knows that!"

"Of course!" said Green Wonder. "Before gardening, Harriet and my mom went into town to run some errands."

"Maybe Harriet forgot Lilly Kitty in the village square!" said Galaxy Gal.

"This is a big clue," said Mega Bear.

"That's why it's going straight into the clue book," said Book Whiz.

"It's also why *we're* going straight to town!" exclaimed Green Wonder.

The Super Cluepers ran to Mr. Mole's store. They found the gumball machine, but not Lilly Kitty.

They looked all around the store, but they could not find her anywhere.

"She's got to be here somewhere," said Green Wonder. He thought and he thought, then he got an idea. "Book Whiz, do you still have Harriet's drawing in the clue book?"

"Yes, here it is," she said.

Green Wonder took the drawing. "If we match up Harriet's drawing with what we see in front of us, we'll know exactly where she was when she drew it!"

"There!" said Galaxy Gal. "She must have drawn it by the gazebo."

When the Super Cluepers got to the gazebo, Lilly Kitty was not there. But Mega Bear found a big hole in the floor. It was dark inside, so Kid Gizmo shone his Looking Light.

"Look!" yelled Green Wonder.

"It's Lilly Kitty," said Galaxy Gal.
"We have to get her out of there," said Book Whiz. "But how?"

"I'll save her!" said Thunder Boy. He quickly crawled inside to where Lilly Kitty was lying.

Thunder Boy tried lifting Lilly Kitty. "She's too heavy," he said.

Green Wonder had an idea. He ran to Mr. Mole's store to borrow an umbrella.

Then he stuck the umbrella in the hole — and pulled out Thunder Boy and Lilly Kitty!

"We solved the mystery!" said Green Wonder.

"Good work, Thunder Boy," said Giggler.

The Super Cluepers brought Lilly Kitty back to Harriet.

"Oh, thank you, Super Cluepers!" she said. "Would you like to stay for tea and some treats? I'm having a tea party."

"Don't mind if we do," said Green Wonder.

"And don't forget about Lilly Kitty," said Galaxy Gal.

"That's right," said Green Wonder. "After all, she's the guest of honor!"

Franklin's
Partner

FRANKLIN had lots of good friends.
They all liked to play the same games.
Their favorite was Bumpy Buggies.

One day, they came up with a great idea.
They would hold a special Bumpy Buggy
race — and everyone in town could join in
the fun!

Franklin and his friends made a poster to promote the big event. Bear hung it up outside Mr. Mole's store.

"A Bumpy Buggy race? That sounds like fun," said Mr. Mole.

"It's going to be *lots* of fun," said Franklin. "But you have to make a buggy."

"And you need to have a partner, too," said Bear. "Every team needs someone at the top to push and someone at the bottom to catch."

81

Franklin and Bear really wanted to win the race. They decided to fix up their old buggy.

"Maybe a new paint job," said Franklin.

"Let's put a siren on top — like an ambulance," added Bear.

"A siren? Aw, Bear. Don't be silly," said Franklin.

Franklin and Bear finally decided that the buggy needed new parts. They knew just where to get them — from Fox's dad.

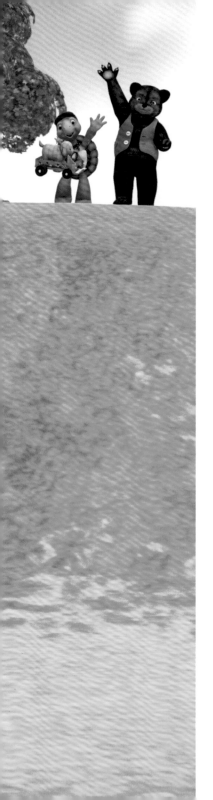

Franklin and Bear went to Fox's house. He and his father were making music with an old chime and a garbage pail.

"Hey, guys!" said Fox. "What are you doing here?"

"We need some new parts for our Bumpy Buggy," said Bear.

"Could we look through your collection of stuff, Mr. Fox?" asked Franklin.

"Sure," said Mr. Fox.

"Come on, Bear," said Franklin. "Let's look for something to make our buggy super cool-io."

"Thanks, Mr. Fox!" said Bear.

Franklin found some blue jar lids. He thought they'd make great new wheels.

"Hey, Bear!" shouted Franklin. "How about these?"

Bear ignored Franklin. He climbed into a bathtub filled with junk. Inside, he found an old airplane.

"Look!" yelled Bear. "Wings! We could make the buggy fly."

"Bear, buggies don't fly," said Franklin.

"We'll try it with wings," said Bear. "If it doesn't look good, we'll do your wheel thing."

Bear attached the green wings to the buggy. "Let's call our buggy the Mean Green Speedmobile," he said.

"The Mean Green Speedmobile?" asked Franklin.

"Yeah," said Bear. "Look, I have to go. You hang on to the Speedmobile."

Franklin grabbed the buggy and frowned. He did not like the changes Bear had made.

Back home, Franklin decided to fix the buggy — the way *he* wanted. As he was putting the finishing touches on it, Bear came to visit.

"What happened?" said Bear. "You took off the wings!"

"It's a rocket now," said Franklin. "And since Sam will ride in it, I've named it Sam's Rocket."

"You even changed the name?" asked Bear.

"It's better this way," said Franklin.

"But, Franklin, we're partners!" said Bear. "That means we decide stuff together."

"*We* didn't decide on wings or 'Mean Green Speedmobile' together," said Franklin. "*You* decided all that stuff."

"If that's what you think, then maybe we shouldn't be partners," shouted Bear.

"Maybe we shouldn't," said Franklin.

Bear stomped out of the shed. He slammed the door shut.

Franklin was upset. He took Sam's Rocket and went for a walk to calm down. At the top of Thrill Hill, Franklin tripped and dropped the buggy. It sped downhill — straight for a big rock!

Suddenly, Bear appeared. He dove onto the path and grabbed the buggy.

Franklin was relieved when he saw the buggy was safe. He got up and ran down to Bear.

"I'm sorry, Bear," said Franklin. "I should have listened to you."

"That's okay, Franklin," said Bear. "I should have listened to you, too."

The two friends shook hands.

"Let's start over," said Franklin. "But this time we'll decide things together. Deal?"

"Deal, partner," said Bear.

The next day, Franklin and Bear arrived at Thrill Hill with their spiffed-up Bumpy Buggy. The two friends had decided to call it Sam's Speedmobile.

All the racers got ready. One partner stood at the starting line. The other partner waited at the finish line.

"Ready! Steady! Go!" yelled Officer Rabbit.

The contestants pushed their buggies, then cheered as they watched them fly down Thrill Hill. It was a close finish, but Goose and Beaver won the race.

"Wasn't that great?" yelled Bear, as he ran down to Franklin.

"Great?" asked Franklin. "We lost!"

"Lost? Who cares?" said Bear. "Did you see how cool-io our buggy looked?"

"You're right, Bear," said Franklin with a laugh. "I never saw a more cool-io buggy in my life!"

Franklin's
Spaceship

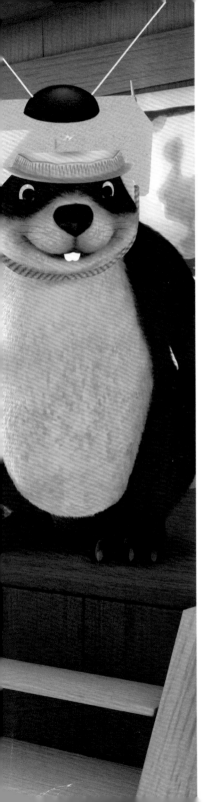

FRANKLIN and his friends had great imaginations. One day, they decided to play astronauts. They dressed up in special space gear and pretended their tree fort was a spaceship.

As they were getting ready to blast off into outer space, Franklin suddenly noticed someone was missing.

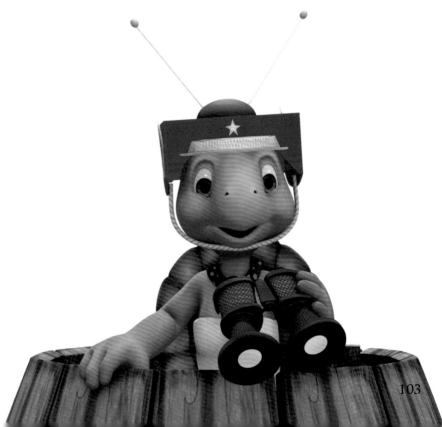

103

"Hold on, everybody!" yelled Franklin. "We forgot about Snail."
Franklin spotted Snail playing his harmonica outside of their tree fort.
"Hey, Snail," said Franklin. "Our spaceship is about to take off.
Climb aboard!"

"Thanks, Franklin," said Snail, "but I'm busy right now. I'm trying to play a song on my harmonica. It goes like this —"

"You can do that later," said Franklin. "We're taking off for Planet Glorp. Come on!"

"Well, okay," said Snail. He slowly climbed aboard the spaceship.

"Welcome aboard, Snail," said Bear. "On this ship, I'm called
Space Bear."

"I'm Moon Beamer," said Beaver.

"Flash Fox, at your service," said Fox.

"Goose the Glorp is my name," said Goose.

"Planet Hopper here," said Rabbit.

"And I'm Captain Star," said Franklin.

Snail looked at his space friends. "That's neat. Who can I be?"

"You can be Robot," said Franklin. "All spaceships need a robot."

"Robot?" said Snail, frowning. "Do I have to be a robot?"

"Yes, and here's your space suit," said Franklin, wrapping him in tinfoil.

"I'd rather practice my new harmonica song," said Snail. "It goes like this —"

"You can do that later," said Franklin. "Your job is to sound the alarm in an emergency. Now let's blast off!"

Franklin and the rest of the crew got ready for takeoff.
"Five, four, three, two, one — blast off!" said Franklin.
Fox and Bear made sounds like an engine. Beaver and Goose shook back and forth in their seats.

Rabbit checked the instrument panel and said, "We are now in outer space!"

Everyone cheered.

"Isn't it cool-io in outer space?" asked Franklin.

"Yes, it is," said Snail. "It makes me want to play a song. It goes like this —"

"You can do that later," said Franklin. "Right now, we have to avoid some giant meteors!"

Franklin accidentally bumped Snail and knocked his harmonica out the spaceship window.

"Oh, no! My harmonica!" said Snail.

"We can get it later," said Franklin. "I need you to sound the emergency!"

"Red alert! Emergency! Danger! Danger!" yelled Snail.

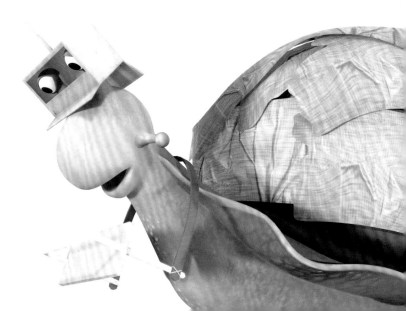

"What's the emergency?" asked Beaver.
"We're going to hit some meteors!" said Franklin.
"What are meteors?" asked Goose.

"They're like giant flying space rocks," explained Franklin.
"What are we going to do?" asked Rabbit.
"Flash Fox! Space Bear! Put the space brakes on!" yelled Franklin.

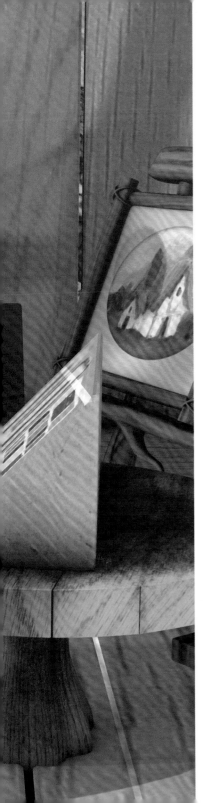

The crew managed to stop their spaceship before they hit the meteors.

"Franklin, can I get my harmonica now that we've stopped?" asked Snail.

"You can do that later," said Franklin. "We still have an emergency!"

"What now?" asked Bear.

"We have to land on Planet Glorp," said Franklin, checking his space chart.

While everyone else ran back to their stations, Snail sighed and slowly crept away. He didn't want to play astronauts anymore.

Franklin and his crew prepared to land on Planet Glorp. Rabbit took the controls and set the spaceship down on land.

"A perfect touchdown!" said Beaver.

"Come on, crew," said Franklin. "Let's check out this planet."

Everyone was ready for action. That's when Franklin noticed that someone was missing.

"Hey, where's Robot Snail?" asked Franklin. They searched the spaceship, but Snail was nowhere to be found.

"He must have gone down to Planet Glorp," said Franklin.

"Why would he do that?" asked Bear.

"I don't know," said Franklin.

"We have to save him," said Goose.

Together, the crew climbed out of the spaceship.

They searched everywhere, but there was no sign of Snail. Then they heard the sound of a harmonica.

"Did you hear that?" asked Franklin. "Come on!"

The friends followed the sound and found Snail in a hollow tree trunk.

"Snail, we were looking all over for you," said Franklin. "Why did you leave?"

"I wanted to play my harmonica, but you wouldn't let me."

"I just wanted you to have fun with us," said Franklin.

"I like playing with you guys, but I also like playing my harmonica," said Snail. "It's fun, too."

"Sorry, Snail," said Franklin. "I guess I didn't think about that. But if you give us another chance, I think I know a way we all can have fun."

"Okay, Franklin," said Snail.

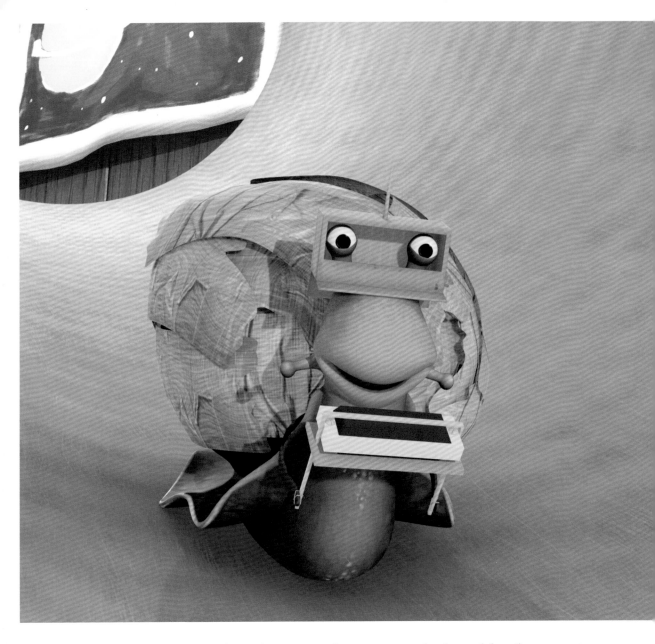

The crew returned to the spaceship. As Snail played his harmonica,
Franklin and his friends sang:

"Blast off! Blast off! Here goes our spaceship!
Blast off! Blast off! For a super space trip!
We'll zoom past the stars, through a comet's tail!
We're on a space adventure with our friend Robot Snail!"

Franklin's
Ups and Downs

FRANKLIN liked playing with his best friend, Bear. And when one of them got a new toy, playing together could be extra fun.

One day, Frankin was building a castle wall for his fish, Goldie, when suddenly Bear bounced past his bedroom window.

"Hey, Franklin!" yelled Bear. "Come see."

Franklin raced outside. He found Bear bouncing around the yard.

"Check it out, Franklin," said Bear. "Pogo Paws!"

"Cool-io! Could I try them?" asked Franklin.

"You bet," said Bear.

Franklin ran to get his safety gear. Bear took off the Pogo Paws. Franklin strapped them onto his feet.

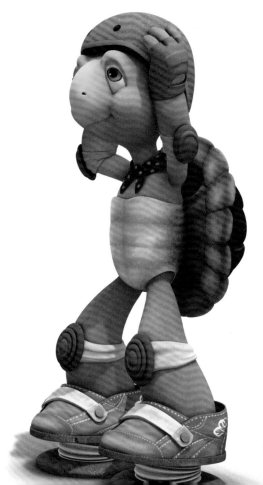

Franklin got up and started to bounce. Once, twice, three times — then he fell on his shell with a thud. The Pogo Paws flew off his feet.

"Sorry," said Bear. "I guess my feet are bigger than yours."

"A lot bigger," said Franklin with a laugh. "I need to get my own cool-io jumping shoes."

That night at dinner, Franklin asked his parents for a pair of Pogo Paws. "We can't buy you everything just because you want it," said his father. "But Pogo Paws are fun," said Franklin.

"Maybe you could work for them," said his father.

"Whenever you finish a special chore, you'll earn a star sticker," added Franklin's mother. "Once you have four, we'll buy the Pogo Paws."

Franklin got right to work.
He pulled weeds from the garden —
and sometimes a carrot!
He cleaned the kitchen so it sparkled.

Franklin put away all the toys in the house.

He even scrubbed Goldie's goldfish bowl until it was spotless.

When Franklin finished his chores, he ran to the chart.

His father counted the stars: "One, two, three, four!"

"You did it!" said Franklin's mother.

"Hooray!" cheered Harriet.

"Yes! Pogo Paws here I come!" said Franklin.

137

The next afternoon, Franklin found his friends in the park. They were all bouncing around on Pogo Paws.

"Look, guys!" shouted Franklin. He held up his new Pogo Paws for everyone to see.

"Show us what you can do," said Rabbit.

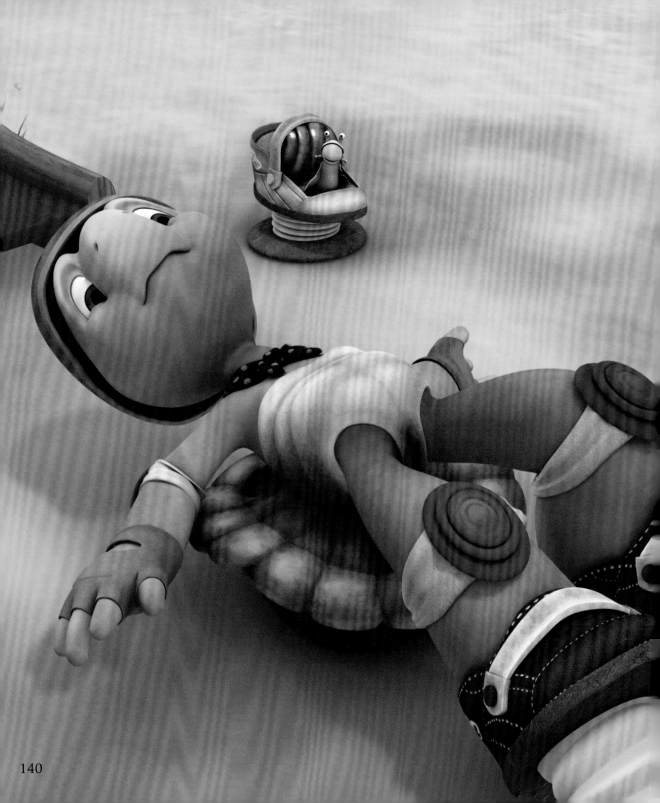

Franklin strapped on his Pogo Paws and got ready.

"One, two, three," said Franklin. He bounced once — then fell on his shell with a thud.

Rabbit, Snail and Fox chuckled.

"It's not nice to laugh at someone just because they can't do something," said Goose.

"Are you all right?" asked Bear, as he helped Franklin to his feet.
"I'm okay," said Franklin with a sigh.

The other friends bounced away, leaving Franklin alone with Bear.
"I must be the clumsiest kid ever," said Franklin sadly.

"You know, when I got my Pogo Paws, I fell down a lot, too," said Bear. "But my mom helped me practice and I got better. Do you want me to help you?"

Franklin thought for a moment. "I'd like that, Bear," he said, smiling.

Together, Franklin and Bear started to bounce slowly. Once, twice, three times.

Then Franklin and Bear started to bounce faster and faster. They bounced all the way to the tree fort.

Beaver, Snail and Goose were playing in the tree fort. When they saw Bear and Franklin, they stopped and stared. They couldn't believe their eyes.

Franklin was bouncing on his Pogo Paws — without falling.
"Yay, Franklin!" they cheered.

"I knew you could do it!" said Bear.
"Thanks," said Franklin. "Now I just need help learning to stop!"

Franklin
in the Stars

FRANKLIN and Harriet loved spending time with their parents. They also loved spending time with their Aunt T.

One night, Franklin and Harriet were very excited. Their parents were going out for dinner — and Aunt T was coming over to babysit.

Franklin and Harriet could hardly wait!

"Hey, everybody," said Aunt T, as she walked in the door.

"Aunt T! Aunt T!" squealed Harriet. "Yay, Aunt T."

Aunt T picked up Harriet and swung her in the air.

"Whee!" shrieked Harriet.

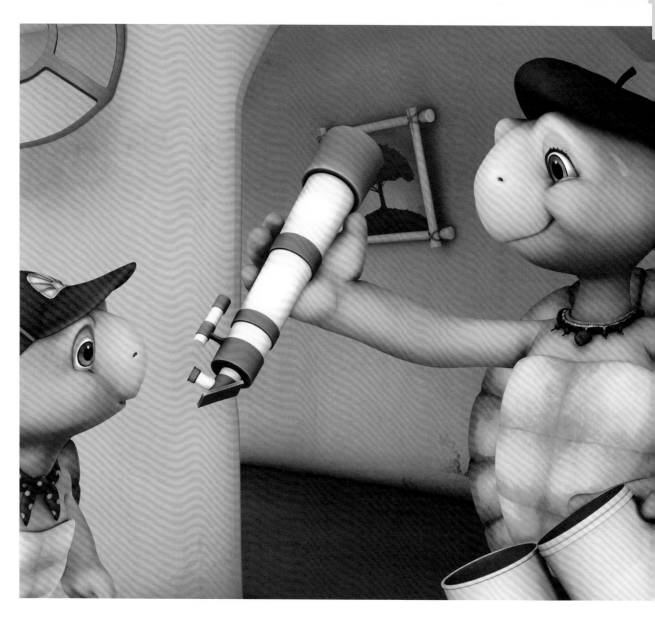

"Hi, Aunt T," said Franklin. He noticed she had a white case in her hand. "What did you bring?"

"Oh, this is my spiffy new telescope," she answered, pulling it out.

"A real telescope? That's so cool-io!" said Franklin.

"A *sillyscope*?" asked Harriet. "Let me see. Let me see!"

"It's a *telescope*, Harriet," said Franklin. "It's for looking at the sky."

"It makes the stars and planets seem really close," said Aunt T. "It's like looking out a spaceship window."

"Can we go outside and try out the telescope?" asked Franklin excitedly.
"You might not be able to see anything in the sky tonight," said
Franklin's father. "I think it's too cloudy."

"Aw," said Franklin with a sigh.

"Cheer up, Franklin," said his mother. "I'm sure Aunt T has something else you can do."

Franklin's parents left for dinner. Franklin looked down at the telescope and frowned. He wanted to look at the night sky more than anything.

"Okay, let the show begin!" exclaimed Aunt T.

"But, Aunt T, we can't even see the stars," said Franklin.

"No stars," said Harriet.

"The whole wide world is a show," said Aunt T. "You just need to find a new way to see it!"

Aunt T took Franklin and Harriet out into the yard. She gave them each a jar. Then she pointed to some lights in the distance.

"Those are fireflies," whispered Aunt T. "I call them 'dancing stars.' Catch them and you'll see why."

Franklin, Harriet and Aunt T caught lots of fireflies. They put them in the jars.

"See?" said Aunt T. "They look just like dancing stars. Let's take them inside."

Once they got inside, Aunt T turned off the lights. Then Franklin, Harriet and Aunt T let the fireflies out of the jars. They flew all around the room.

"Pretty stars!" said Harriet.

"Neat-o," said Franklin. "It does feel like outer space in here!"

"What else would you see in outer space?" asked Aunt T.
"Spaceships!" said Franklin.
"Vroom, vroom!" shouted Harriet.

"You think you could make a spaceship?" asked Aunt T.

"Sure we could!" exclaimed Franklin.

Franklin made his spaceship out of his toy trunk. Harriet made hers out of a laundry basket.

Franklin and Harriet were ready to blast off into outer space. There were just a few things missing.

Franklin gathered a bunch of balls. He painted his soccer ball brown for the planet Mercury. He painted another ball blue for Venus.

Harriet painted a beach ball yellow for the Sun.

Aunt T painted another ball with stripes. Then Franklin put rings on it for Saturn.

And for the Moon, Franklin found a glow-in-the-dark ball!

167

When Mr. and Mrs. Turtle came home from dinner that night, they couldn't believe their eyes.

It was as if they had entered outer space!

"Wow!" said Franklin's mother.

"I know," said Aunt T with a laugh. "It's out of this world."

"Way, way out," said Franklin's father.

"Come look at Saturn," said Franklin. "It's got rings and everything!"

"I've certainly never seen Saturn up close like this before," replied his father.

"That's because you've never been to outer space," said Franklin.

Just then, a firefly flew past.

"Oh, look!" said Franklin's mother. "There's a shooting star. Make a wish, Franklin."

Franklin closed his eyes.

"I wish for cloudy nights every time Aunt T comes over!"

Franklin
and the Gecko Games

FRANKLIN and his friends were in a special club called the Nature Nuts.
Mr. Owl was their club leader.

He taught them about the wonders of nature — and about the club's
pet lizard, Gordon.

"Gordon the gecko is an insectivore," said Mr. Owl. "That means he likes to eat insects."

"Does that make me a cookievore?" asked Bear.

Everyone laughed.

"I suppose so," said Mr. Owl.

"Now, Nature Nuts, we have some club business," continued Mr. Owl. "Summer holidays are coming, and Gordon will need a gecko-sitter. Any volunteers?"

Franklin loved pets. He thought about his fish, Goldie, and smiled. He thought it would be fun to gecko-sit.

Franklin raised his hand to volunteer. So did Beaver.
"Let's take a vote," suggested Mr. Owl.
Rabbit, Snail and Goose voted for Beaver.
Bear, Fox and Goose voted for Franklin.

"Goose! You can't vote twice!" said Beaver. "Everyone knows that."

"But I can't decide," said Goose.

"There's no rush. Think it over," said Mr. Owl. "Now let's do the Nature Nuts pledge."

They placed a hand over their hearts.

"Winter, summer, spring and fall!
We love nature, one and all!
We're the Nuts! We're the Nuts!
We're the Nature, Nature Nuts!
Yay, Nature!"

Soon it was Gordon's nap time.

"Goose, you can tell me your vote later," said Mr. Owl, as he took Gordon back inside the school.

"Why wait, Goose?" said Rabbit once Mr. Owl was gone. "We know you're going to vote for Beaver."

"Yeah, you're best friends," added Bear.

"I wouldn't vote for Beaver just because we're best friends," said Goose. "I'll pick the person I think will do the best job."

"How are you going to decide that?" asked Bear.

That's when Goose had an idea. They would hold a competition —
special Gecko Games — to decide. Goose looked in her book about
geckos to come up with an idea for the first game.

"I've got it!" she said. She gave Franklin and Beaver one jar each.
"What's this for?" asked Beaver.
"The Grasshopper Catch," said Goose. "Gordon eats lots of grasshoppers. We'll have a race to see who can catch the most!"

"A race? I'm not ready to race," said Beaver. But it was too late.
"Get ready! Get set! Go!" yelled Goose.

Franklin and Beaver ran around the park. They scooped up as many grasshoppers as they could find until Goose yelled for them to stop.

She counted the grasshoppers in each jar. Franklin had six. Beaver had five. Franklin won the first Gecko Game!

Next, Goose decided to hold a Gecko Quiz.

"Do geckos like their tanks hot or cold?" asked Goose.

Beaver honked her bicycle horn. "Hot! Geckos like their tanks hot," said Beaver.

"Right," said Goose. "One point for Beaver. Now, do geckos like to play at night or during the day?"

Beaver honked her bicycle horn again. "Day!" she shouted.

"Wrong," said Franklin. "It depends on the kind of gecko. Right, Goose?"

"Right," said Goose. "One point for Franklin — we have a tie! The next question will decide who wins this game."

Goose thought of a really hard question.
"What do you call the tiny hairs on a gecko's feet?" asked Goose.
Beaver honked her horn. "Setae!" she said.

"Right you are," said Goose. "You won the Gecko Quiz!"

Franklin and Beaver had won one game each. Goose needed to come up with one more game to break the tie.

Goose decided on a game of Gecko Hide-and-Seek. Snail dressed up like a gecko and hid. Whoever found Snail would win the Gecko Games!

Beaver and Franklin started searching. They searched and searched, but they could not find Snail.

"We've looked everywhere!" said Beaver, as she flopped down on a nearby tire swing.

"Whoa!" yelled Snail.
Beaver jumped off the tire swing. She had almost squashed Snail!
Franklin ran over and picked up Snail. "I won!"

"Maybe it *is* better if you take care of Gordon," said Beaver. "I'd never forgive myself if I hurt him the way I almost hurt Snail."

Franklin watched as Beaver started to walk away. He didn't feel like a winner at all.

Just then, Mr. Owl came outside with the gecko. "Goose, did you decide who gets to look after Gordon?" he asked.

"Yes. The winner is Fra—"

"Wait!" said Franklin.

Franklin thought about Goldie and how lucky he was to already have a pet. "I think Beaver should take Gordon."

"Really?" said Beaver.

"Beaver will do a great job," explained Franklin. "She's not just smart — she's pet smart!"

"Thanks, Franklin!" said Beaver. "I'll be the best gecko-sitter ever."